For Elizabeth

Copyright © 1987–2016 by Martin Handford

First U.S. edition 2009

Library of Congress Cataloging-in-Publication Data is available.

Library of Congress Catalog Card Number 2009012055

ISBN 978-0-7636-4689-9

18 19 20 21 22 SWT 8 7 6 5 4 3 2

Printed in Dongguan, Guangdong, China

This book was typeset in Optima and Wallyfont.
The illustrations were done in ink and watercolor or in ink and colored digitally.

Candlewick Press
99 Dover Street
Somerville, Massachusetts 02144

visit us at www.candlewick.com

WHERE'S WALDO?

THE INCREDIBLE PAPER CHASE

MARTIN HANDFORD

CANDLEWICK PRESS

THE JURASSIC GAMES

GOODNESS CRETACEOUS! WHO WILL YOU SUPPORT FROM THE SIDELINES: THE BLUE STRIPY-SAURUS TEAM OR THE PINK SPOTTY-DOCUS TEAM? WILL YOU CHEER FOR CRICKET, ROWING, OR BASKETBALL? DON'T FORGET TO WAVE IF YOU SEE A T. REX — THEY'RE NOT ON ANY TEAM, BUT YOU WOULDN'T WANT TO GET ON THEIR BAD SIDE!

PICTURE THIS

PHEW! LOOK AT ALL THESE FRAMED PORTRAITS. ALTHOUGH THEY MAY BE COLORED DIFFERENTLY, SOME OF THESE ARE CHARACTERS I HAVE MET ON MY OTHER TRAVELS. THERE ARE ALSO SOME WHO APPEAR ELSEWHERE IN THIS BOOK. CAN YOU SPOT FOUR CHARACTERS THAT APPEAR TWICE IN THIS SPECTACULAR DISPLAY?

MUDDY SWAMPY JUNGLE GAME

FOLD OUT THE PAGES AND FOLLOW THE INTREPID EXPLORERS THROUGH THE SLUDGY SWAMP! WATCH OUT FOR PIRANHAS AND MONSTERS OF THE DEEP AS YOU GO!

How to play the game:

★ Find some players (up to nine) and a die.

★ Press out the counters and Waldo cards.

★ Take turns rolling the die and moving your counters along the board. Follow the instructions you find each time you land.

★ The first to land on FINISH is the winner. (If the number you throw is too high, count to FINISH and back, and try again on your next turn.)

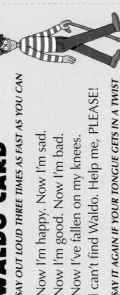

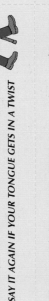

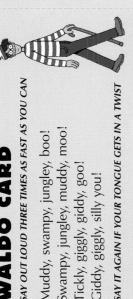

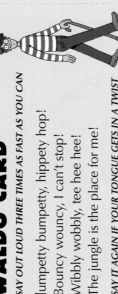
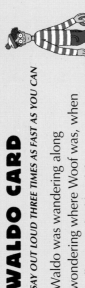
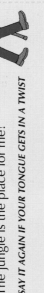

WALDO CARD
SAY OUT LOUD THREE TIMES AS FAST AS YOU CAN

Waldo! Wow! Phew! Fantastic!
Groovy! Brilliant! Waldo-tastic!
Super! Wizard! Spiffing! Cool!
Wish this was a swimming pool!

SAY IT AGAIN IF YOUR TONGUE GETS IN A TWIST

WALDO CARD
SAY OUT LOUD THREE TIMES AS FAST AS YOU CAN

Waldo and Woof went walking
in a wonderfully wild, wet wood.
They watched a woodpecker whistle
where a woolly mammoth once stood!

SAY IT AGAIN IF YOUR TONGUE GETS IN A TWIST

WALDO CARD
SAY OUT LOUD THREE TIMES AS FAST AS YOU CAN

What a whopping shock it was
for all the other Waldos when
the one and only real Waldo
walked into Waldoland!

SAY IT AGAIN IF YOUR TONGUE GETS IN A TWIST

WALDO CARD
SAY OUT LOUD THREE TIMES AS FAST AS YOU CAN

Which days does Waldo say are his
holidays? Moonday, Toesday, Friendsday,
Thirstyday, Cryday, Chitterchatterday.
It's fantastic-wow-what-a-lot-of-fun-day!

SAY IT AGAIN IF YOUR TONGUE GETS IN A TWIST

WALDO CARD
SAY OUT LOUD THREE TIMES AS FAST AS YOU CAN

It's incredible! Wow! I say!
What a spiffing Waldo day!
Sing this simply super song –
Crash! Tinkle! Bing bang bong!

SAY IT AGAIN IF YOUR TONGUE GETS IN A TWIST

WALDO CARD
SAY OUT LOUD THREE TIMES AS FAST AS YOU CAN

Muddy, swampy, jungley, boo!
Swampy, jungley, muddy, moo!
Tickly, giggly, giddy, goo!
Giddy, giggly, silly you!

SAY IT AGAIN IF YOUR TONGUE GETS IN A TWIST

WALDO CARD
SAY OUT LOUD THREE TIMES AS FAST AS YOU CAN

Waldo was wandering along
wondering where Woof was, when
Odlaw sneaked by slyly,
suddenly slipping in the sludgy swamp!

SAY IT AGAIN IF YOUR TONGUE GETS IN A TWIST

WALDO CARD
SAY OUT LOUD THREE TIMES AS FAST AS YOU CAN

Jumpetty bumpetty, hippety hop!
Bouncy wouncy, I can't stop!
Wibbly wobbly, tee hee hee!
The jungle is the place for me!

SAY IT AGAIN IF YOUR TONGUE GETS IN A TWIST

WALDO CARD
SAY OUT LOUD THREE TIMES AS FAST AS YOU CAN

Now I'm happy. Now I'm sad.
Now I'm good. Now I'm bad.
Now I've fallen on my knees.
I can't find Waldo. Help me, PLEASE!

SAY IT AGAIN IF YOUR TONGUE GETS IN A TWIST

WALDO CARD
SAY OUT LOUD THREE TIMES AS FAST AS YOU CAN

If Waldo wants Woof when
Wenda wants Woof, who will
Woof woof-woof at when Wizard
Whitebeard wants Woof? Bow-wow!

SAY IT AGAIN IF YOUR TONGUE GETS IN A TWIST

11

12

13 Boo hoo! You're missing your teddy bear! Suck your thumb and miss a turn.

14

15 Pow! Take a Waldo card!

16

17 Boo! Hiss! You are the cleanest, tidiest person in the jungle! Mess up your hair! Miss a turn.

10 Oops! You disturb a pink-spotted rhino baby – and its mother! Say sorry 17 times! Go back 4.

21 Oh, woe! You take a wrong turn! Have a good cry! Go back 9.

20 Phew! A water buffalo is besotted with you! Bellow as loudly as you can! Go forward 2.

19

18 Hurrah! You are the grubbiest, scruffiest person ever! Take 14 bows! Go forward 4.

9 Wham bam! Take a Waldo card.

22 Pow! Take a Waldo card!

23

45 Phew! Take a Waldo card!

46 Crrrash! You chop down a tree in your way. Flex your muscles! Take another turn.

47 Smash! A tree falls on you! Get everyone to hug you better! Miss a turn.

24 Wop wallop! Take a Waldo card.

44 Bzzz bzzz! Bees show you a shortcut! Buzz long and loud! Go forward 6.

49 Phew! Take a Waldo card!

48

40 Thump! Whump! You are attacked by beastly boars! Run 6 times around the room! Go back 16!

43

50

42 Wozzy woo! Take a Waldo card!

41

51

52 Oh, no! Your map is upside down! Make a funny face! Go back 4.

53

FINISH

WHAT A DOG FIGHT!
BOW WOW WOW! TWO ARMIES
ARE LOCKED IN BATTLE, ALL WITH
DOG MASKS ON. ONE ARMY IS DRESSED
IN BLUE, BLACK, AND WHITE, AND THE
OTHER IN RED, BROWN, AND CREAM. CAN
YOU FIND EIGHT SOLDIERS, FOUR FROM
EACH SIDE, WITH SOMETHING IN ONE OF
THE OTHER SIDE'S COLORS? OH, AND
WHERE IS WOOF IN THIS DOG PACK?

THE ENORMOUS PARTY
WOW! HOW EXCITING! ARE YOU IN THE MOOD FOR A PARTY, WALDO-WATCHERS? LOOK AT THE BALLOONS, THE STREAMERS, AND ALL THE SMILING FACES! THE FLAGS OF 18 COUNTRIES ARE FLYING HERE — CAN YOU SPOT SIX FLAGS THAT HAVE SOMETHING WRONG WITH THEM? *

* THE ANSWERS ARE AT THE BACK OF THIS BOOK. NO CHEATING!

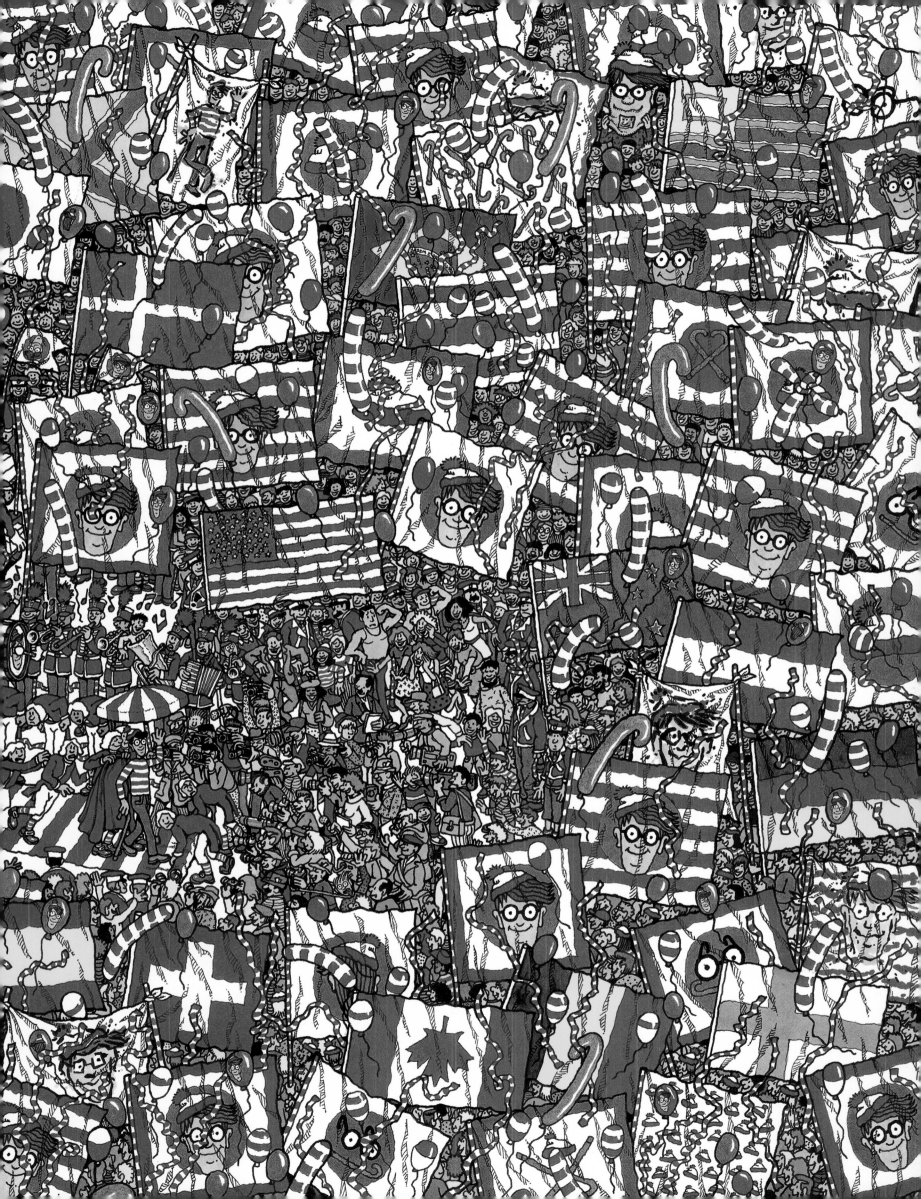

WHERE'S WALDO?
THE INCREDIBLE PAPER CHASE CHECKLIST

THE CASTLE SIEGE

- [ ] Five blue-coated soldiers wearing blue plumes
- [ ] Five red-coated soldiers wearing red plumes
- [ ] A blue-coated soldier wearing a red plume
- [ ] A red-coated soldier wearing a blue plume
- [ ] Four blue-coated archers
- [ ] Five characters holding white feathers
- [ ] Some pike men holding pikes
- [ ] Minors digging a tunnel
- [ ] Twenty-two ladders
- [ ] Some longbowmen wearing long bows
- [ ] Five catapults
- [ ] Twenty-seven ladies dressed in blue
- [ ] Twelve men with white beards
- [ ] A wishing well
- [ ] Two tidy witches
- [ ] Nine blue shields
- [ ] Four horses
- [ ] Three round red shields
- [ ] A prisoner in a puzzling position
- [ ] Eight men snoozing
- [ ] Someone with by far the longest hair
- [ ] A soldier with one bare foot
- [ ] Eighteen characters with their tongues out
- [ ] Five tents

THE JURASSIC GAMES

- [ ] A dinosaur volleyball game
- [ ] A dinosaur rowing race
- [ ] Dinosaurs playing cricket
- [ ] A dinosaur soccer match
- [ ] A dinosaur windsurfer race
- [ ] Dinosaurs playing baseball
- [ ] A dinosaur football game
- [ ] Dinosaurs playing basketball
- [ ] Dinosaurs playing golf
- [ ] A dinosaur steeplechase race
- [ ] A dinosaur polo match
- [ ] Four sets of dinosaur cheerleaders
- [ ] Dinosaurs keeping score with their tails
- [ ] Some show-jumping dinosaurs

PICTURE THIS

- [ ] A bird escaped from its frame
- [ ] An angry dragon
- [ ] An airplane with real wings
- [ ] An alarm clock
- [ ] A running cactus
- [ ] A rude tree trunk
- [ ] Some fish fingers
- [ ] A mermaid in reverse
- [ ] Three skiers
- [ ] A messy eater
- [ ] An upside-down picture
- [ ] A giant foot
- [ ] Three romantic animals
- [ ] A foot being tickled
- [ ] A picture within a picture
- [ ] Two men sharing the same hat
- [ ] Two helmets worn back-to-front
- [ ] Someone drinking through a straw
- [ ] Three flags
- [ ] Nine tongues hanging out
- [ ] A caveman escaped from his frame
- [ ] Seven dogs and a dogfish
- [ ] A bandaged finger
- [ ] A braided mustache
- [ ] Four bears
- [ ] Three helmets with red plumes
- [ ] Four cats
- [ ] Four ducks
- [ ] Yellow, blue, and red picture frames

THE GREAT RETREAT

- [ ] A shield suddenly vacated
- [ ] A heart on a soldier's tunic
- [ ] One curved sword
- [ ] A soldier carrying a hammer
- [ ] One striped spear
- [ ] A soldier not wearing a top
- [ ] Two runaway boots
- [ ] A horseless rider
- [ ] A soldier with a sword and an ax
- [ ] Three bare feet
- [ ] Four pink tails
- [ ] A spear with tips at both ends
- [ ] A helmet with a blue plume
- [ ] A soldier with a red boot and a blue boot
- [ ] A helmet with a red plume

MUDDY SWAMPY JUNGLE GAME

- [ ] An explorer with long sleeves
- [ ] An explorer carrying two spears
- [ ] An explorer wearing a shoe
- [ ] Four contented frogs
- [ ] An explorer with a white beard
- [ ] Five explorers not wearing tops
- [ ] A toe being nipped
- [ ] An explorer wearing a curled-up snake
- [ ] A belt buckled at the back
- [ ] An explorer with two cross-belts
- [ ] Ten butterflies
- [ ] A spear with tips at both ends
- [ ] Eight explorers pointing and laughing
- [ ] Three snapped spears

WHAT A DOG FIGHT!

- [ ] A gundog soldier
- [ ] A guard-dog soldier
- [ ] A boxer-dog soldier
- [ ] A bloodhound soldier
- [ ] A Great Dane soldier
- [ ] A prize poodle soldier
- [ ] Two soldiers begging for bones
- [ ] Two soldiers running to fetch a ball
- [ ] Four stars on one tunic
- [ ] A dog basket
- [ ] A dog wearing a man mask
- [ ] Two fellow soldiers fighting each other
- [ ] Four ticklish feet
- [ ] A howling dog soldier
- [ ] A soldier with two tails
- [ ] A white star on a cream tunic
- [ ] Cream eyes on a white dog mask
- [ ] A soldier with a black leg and a brown leg
- [ ] A soldier with a black arm and a cream arm
- [ ] A cream glove on a blue striped arm
- [ ] A cream glove on a black striped arm
- [ ] A brown dog mask on a blue tunic
- [ ] A blue nose on a brown dog mask

THE BEAT OF THE DRUMS

- [ ] A rude back row
- [ ] Courtesy causing a pile-up
- [ ] Some very short spears
- [ ] A group facing in all directions
- [ ] A collision about to happen
- [ ] A domino effect
- [ ] Spears held upside down
- [ ] A never-ending spear
- [ ] Two hats joined together
- [ ] Some very scruffy soldiers
- [ ] A soldier wearing only one shoe
- [ ] A soldier wearing red shoes
- [ ] Thirty-five horses
- [ ] A pink hatband and a blue hatband
- [ ] One blue spear
- [ ] One lost shoe
- [ ] One hat with a yellow feather
- [ ] One hat with a red hatband

THE GREAT ESCAPE

- [ ] Ten men wearing green hoods
- [ ] Ten men wearing only one glove
- [ ] Ten men wearing hoods not matching gloves
- [ ] Ten men wearing two different colored gloves
- [ ] Ten men wearing short and long gloves
- [ ] Ten lost gloves
- [ ] Ten men wearing one fingerless glove
- [ ] Six ladders
- [ ] Nineteen shovels
- [ ] Five question mark shapes formed by the hedge

THE ENORMOUS PARTY

- [ ] Five back views of Waldo's head
- [ ] A servant bending over backward
- [ ] Two muscle-men being ignored
- [ ] An eight-man band
- [ ] A punctured tire
- [ ] A helmet worn backward
- [ ] Eight front wheels
- [ ] Two upside-down faces of Waldo
- [ ] A biker without a motorbike
- [ ] Seven red boots
- [ ] A man wrapped in a streamer
- [ ] A uniform that is too small
- [ ] A uniform that is too big
- [ ] Two men on one motorbike
- [ ] Someone wearing a red tie
- [ ] Someone wearing a blue beret
- [ ] A reluctant arm-rest

THE WACKY WALDO CIRCUS

- [ ] Four reluctant human cannonballs
- [ ] A clown wearing five hats
- [ ] A clown with a big honker
- [ ] A bandsman playing bagpipes
- [ ] A bespectacled family of four
- [ ] A bow tie in a clown's hair
- [ ] An icy ice-pop seller
- [ ] One man supporting three
- [ ] Three straws in one cup
- [ ] Two thirsty clowns
- [ ] A clown being used as a broom
- [ ] Three ketchup victims
- [ ] A boy with three drinks
- [ ] A man with six drinks
- [ ] Twelve clowns with flowers in their hats

THE ENORMOUS PARTY – ANSWERS

		FLAGS WITH FAULTS
1 France	10 Switzerland	3 Diagonal red stripes missing
2 The Netherlands	11 U.S.A.	4 Flying backward
3 United Kingdom	12 Canada	5 One star missing
4 Sweden	13 Belgium	11 Red and white stripes reversed
5 Australia	14 New Zealand	12 Maple leaf upside-down
6 Norway	15 Finland	14 Diagonal red stripes missing
7 Spain	16 Austria	
8 Japan	17 Germany	
9 Denmark	18 Brazil	

PENCIL AND PAPER

Did you find the ten tiny pieces of paper that Waldo dropped from his notepad — one in every scene? Waldo has also left his pencil somewhere on the journey — can you go back and find it, super-seekers?

AND TWO MORE THINGS!

Dozens of Waldo-watchers appear in this book (there is at least one in every scene, but some scenes have many more!).

There's another character — apart from Waldo, Woof, Wenda, Wizard Whitebeard, and Odlaw — in every scene. Can you find her?

STEP RIGHT UP! STEP RIGHT UP!
Be happy! Jump for joy!
Dance a dizzy dance!

The Wacky Waldo Circus
is in town!

THE WACKY WALDO CIRCUS
THE FOLLOWING PAGES ARE PURELY
FOR YOUR DELIGHT! FOLD OUT THE
PAGES AND PRESS OUT THE ACROBATS,
THE CLOWNS, AND THE PUPPETEERS....
TO PUT THE CIRCUS TOGETHER, LOOK
INSIDE THE ENVELOPE FOR HELP. NOW
INVITE YOUR FRIENDS, FAMILY, AND
PETS TO TAKE THEIR SEATS — THE
MORE, THE MERRIER! THEN STRIKE
UP THE BAND, HAND OUT THE
POPCORN, AND PUT ON YOUR
VERY OWN SHOW! WOW!